The
Princess
and the He

Karen Wallace
Illustrated by Miriam Latimer

A & C Black • London

White Wolves series consultant: Sue Ellis,
Centre for Literacy in Primary Education

This book can be used in the White Wolves Guided Reading
programme by readers of average ability in Year 2

First paperback edition 2010
First published 2009 by
A & C Black Publishers Ltd
36 Soho Square, London, W1D 3QY

www.acblack.com

Text copyright © 2009 Karen Wallace
Illustrations copyright © 2009 Miriam Latimer

The rights of Karen Wallace and Miriam Latimer to be identified
as the author and illustrator of this work has been asserted by them
in accordance with the Copyrights, Designs and Patents Act 1988.

ISBN 978-1-4081-2217-4

A CIP catalogue for this book is available from the British Library.

Printed and bound in China

Chapter One

Once there was a princess called Jules. She had all she wanted, except for one thing.

Princess Jules did *not* have a *real* prince, so she could live happily ever after.

He had to look like a film star...

cook like a chef...

and dance like a dream...

Above all, her prince had to say nice things to her, *no matter what.*

But where would she find him?

And how would she know if he was a *real* prince or not?

"Put a message on the internet," said King Flash.

"Then invite them to the castle," said Queen Glitter. "But whatever they tell you, make them prove it."

Princess Jules sent out a message on her computer.

WANTED! A REAL PRINCE FOR A REAL PRINCESS.

She curled up with her book and waited for the doorbell to ring.

Chapter Two

The first prince was called Desmond.
He said he was a brilliant cook.

Princess Jules remembered her mother's warning. "Make me something delicious," she demanded.

Prince Desmond shook like a jelly. "Sorry," he muttered. "I just remembered I'm late for something." And he ran off.

Later, Princess Jules found out that Desmond worked as a waiter and wasn't a real prince at all.

The next prince said he was a dancing champion. But when Princess Jules put on some music, he stepped on her foot and nearly broke her toe.

So she said goodbye to him, too.

Just then, a helicopter landed outside. Princess Jules looked through the window. A gorgeous prince was waving at her!

A minute later, Prince Ferdinand danced through the door holding a silver tray. On it was an ice-cream sundae and a silver spoon.

Princess Jules was delighted. She had found her *real* prince at last!

But, as she picked up the spoon, Prince Ferdinand picked up her book with a frown.

"What's wrong?" asked Princess Jules.

"I don't like princesses who read," said the prince. "They think they're *so* smart."

"Then I suggest you buzz off," said Princess Jules. "*Real* princes don't talk like that."

Poor Princess Jules was fed up.

"I'll never find a real prince," she sighed.

Two fat tears rolled down her face.

Chapter Three

It was a stormy night. Thunder and
lightning crashed and flashed around
the castle.

Queen Glitter made hamburgers
and they sat down to watch a film called
The Pirate Princess.

But Princess Jules was miserable.
"I'm going to bed," she sniffed. "And I'm
not getting up in the morning."

"Don't be silly," said King Flash.
"Everything will be OK."

"No, it won't," replied Princess Jules
sadly.

Around midnight, a banging noise filled the castle.

"Wake up," cried Queen Glitter. "Someone's at the door!"

A moment later, the king and queen were standing in the front hall.

They were staring at a young man who looked like he'd been through a washing machine.

"Who are you?" asked King Flash.

"I don't know," said the young man.
"I slipped in the mud and hit my head
on a rock." He rubbed his ear. "I don't
remember anything."

"I think he's a tramp," whispered Queen
Glitter.

But King Flash felt sorry for the stranger.
"You can spend the night with us," he said.

The young man bowed. "Thank you,"
he said. "That's very kind."

There was something about the way he bowed… Queen Glitter changed her mind. Maybe he wasn't a tramp after all.

"Leave this to me," she said.

Queen Glitter led the stranger to their best bedroom. It had a four-poster bed with four mattresses piled on top of each other.

When the young man wasn't looking, she put a pearl earring under the third mattress.

Chapter Four

The next morning, the young man was so stiff, he could hardly move. As he tried to get out of bed, he fell. *Whack*! His head hit the floor and his memory came back.

He was called Prince George and he had come to find a *real* princess.

Then his Rolls Royce had broken down, so he had started to walk, slipped in the mud and hit his head.

But who was going to believe him?

There was a knock at the door. Queen Glitter and King Flash appeared.

"How did you sleep?" asked the queen.

Prince George went pink. He knew it was wrong to lie.

"Badly," he said. "But let me introduce myself. My name is Prince George and I am here to meet your daughter."

Queen Glitter looked at King Flash.

"How *badly* did you sleep?" she asked.

"Very badly," replied Prince George. "I'm black and blue all over."

The king and queen were delighted. They gave the prince clean clothes and led him downstairs.

Chapter Five

Princess Jules was in the kitchen when the door opened.

"This is Prince George," said Queen Glitter, smiling. "He wants to cook you breakfast."

Five minutes later, Princess Jules was eating boiled eggs with runny yolks, just the way she liked them. What's more, Prince George was completely gorgeous.

Princess Jules sat back. "Why are you here?" she asked.

So Prince George explained he was looking for a *real* princess. Someone who loved watching films ... eating good food...

And dancing at parties.

Above all, he wanted someone who said nice things, *no matter what.* Princess Jules was perfect.

Everything Prince George said *sounded* true. But Princess Jules had to be sure.

"Can you *prove* you're a real prince?" she asked.

"Of *course* he's a real prince!" shouted Queen Glitter, who had been listening at the door. "Last night I put a pearl earring under *three* mattresses. This morning he woke up black and blue all over!"

"Only a *real* prince is that sensitive," said King Glitter.

It was a dream come true! Princess Jules jumped up and threw her arms around Prince George.

"You're the one for me!" she cried.

Prince George held her tight. "And you're the one for me!"

Princess Jules and Prince George were married at once. It was a wonderful wedding. The food was delicious and everyone danced all night.

And, of course, they lived happily ever after, because they always said nice things to each other, *no matter what!*